1915

E
Rob   Roberts, Sarah

          I want to go home!

Sesame Street Start-to-Read Books™
help young children take a giant step into reading.
The stories have been skillfully written, designed,
and illustrated to provide funny, satisfying
reading experiences for the child just starting out.
Let Big Bird, Bert and Ernie, Oscar the Grouch,
and all the Sesame Street Muppets get your child
into reading early with these wonderful stories!

Library of Congress Cataloging in Publication Data:
Roberts, Sarah. I want to go home! (A Sesame Street start-to-read book) SUMMARY: Big Bird goes to stay with his grandmother
at the beach and is homesick until he makes a new friend.
1. Children's stories, American. [1. Grandmothers—Fiction. 2. Homesickness—Fiction. 3. Puppets—Fiction]
I. Mathieu, Joseph. II. Series: Sesame Street start-to-read books. PZ7.R54428Iad 1985 [E] 84-11725
ISBN: 0-394-87027-1 (trade); 0-394-97027-6 (lib. bdg.) Manufactured in the United States of America 1 2 3 4 5 6 7 8 9 0

A Sesame Street Start-to-Read Book™

I Want to Go Home!

by Sarah Roberts • illustrated by Joe Mathieu

Featuring Jim Henson's Sesame Street Muppets

Random House / Children's Television Workshop

Today was a big day for Big Bird.
He was going to visit Granny Bird.
She lived at the seashore!
It was his first trip
away from home.

Big Bird's friends took him
to the bus stop.
"Good-bye, Big Bird! Have fun!
We will miss you," they said.
"I will miss you, too," he said.

Big Bird thought the bus
would never get there.
"Gee, I hope Granny is waiting
for me," he said to himself.

At last the bus stopped.

Granny Bird waved to Big Bird.

"My little Big Bird!

I am so happy to see you!"

Granny said.

"Me, too, Granny!" Big Bird said.

After lunch they went to the beach.
Granny's friends all said,
"My, what a nice grandson!"
But Big Bird did not want to talk.
He wanted to go into the water.
"Go on, dear," said Granny.
"I can watch you from here."

Big Bird ran to the water.
It was the first time
that he had ever seen the sea.
"Wow! It sure is big!" he said.
He had fun all afternoon
racing the waves
and playing in the sand.

Granny and Big Bird had supper
on the porch.
They watched the sun go down.
Big Bird yawned.
"Time for bed," Granny said.

Granny tucked him in,
kissed him good night,
and turned on the night light.
"Sleep tight," she said.

But Big Bird did not sleep tight.
He thought about Sesame Street.
And the more he thought,
the sadder he felt.
"I miss my nest," he whispered.

A tear rolled down his cheek.
"I miss my friends,"
he cried softly.
"I want to go HOME!"
He cried himself to sleep.

At breakfast Big Bird just looked
at his birdseed pancakes.
"What is wrong, Big Bird?"
Granny asked.
"When will I be going home?"
Big Bird asked sadly.
"I know what is wrong.
You are homesick!"
Granny said.
"Will I have to go to a doctor?"
Big Bird asked.
"No, Big Bird," Granny said.
"You will get better
all by yourself—and very soon."

Then Granny gave Big Bird
some picture postcards.
"Do you want to send these
to your friends back home?"
she asked.

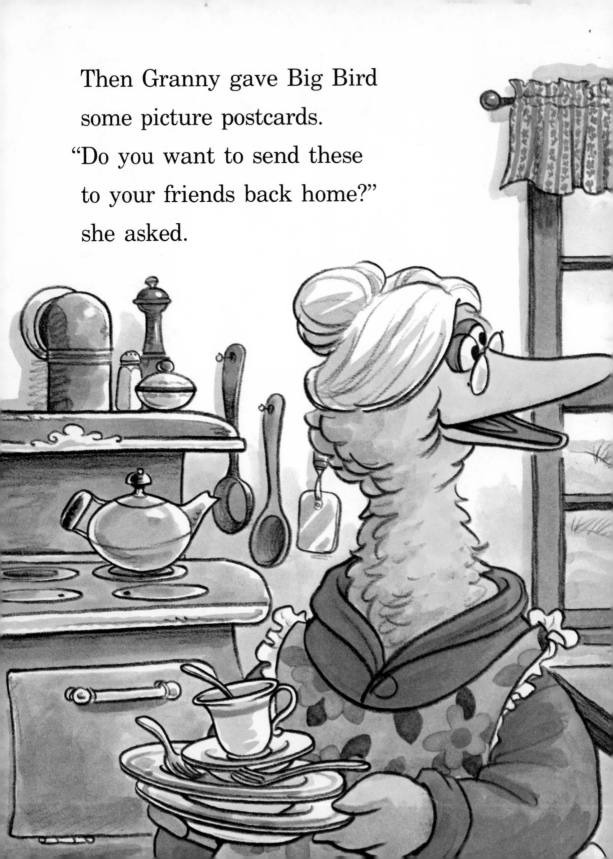

"Yes!" Big Bird said happily.
"You write what I say
and I will write my name myself."

They mailed the postcards
on their way to the beach.
Then Big Bird said,
"I am going to build
a Sesame Street sandcastle!"

He got his pail and shovel
and started to dig.
He worked and worked.
At last it was built.
"Look, Granny, I live here
and Ernie and Bert live there
and—"

Just then a big wave
crashed onto the beach.
It rolled over
Big Bird's wonderful sandcastle.

"Oh, what a shame!" Granny said.
"But don't cry, Big Bird.
Why don't you try to find
some pretty sea shells
to give to your friends?"

Big Bird walked down the beach.
He found a big shell for Ernie,
a little spotted shell for Bert,
and a round shell that looked
like a cookie.
"This one is for Cookie Monster,"
he said.
Thinking of his friends back home
made Big Bird feel homesick again.

Then Big Bird saw something funny—
a soggy old boot.
He picked it up.
And someone laughed.
Big Bird looked around
and saw a boy.

"What are you going to do
with that rotten old boot?"
the boy asked Big Bird.
"Give it to Oscar!"
said Big Bird.
And he told the boy about
his friend Oscar the Grouch,
who liked everything yucchy.

The boy's name was Wally.
He lived in town.
"Come on," he said.
"I'll show you my secret cave!"

"Wow!" Big Bird said.
"Snuffy would love your cave!"
Then Big Bird told Wally
about his friend Snuffy.
"I wish I had a friend
like that!" Wally said.

That night Big Bird ate two bowls
of birdseed stew for supper.
He told Granny all about
his new friend Wally.
Granny said, "I am so happy
that you feel better."

Later, in bed, Big Bird missed
his nest a little bit.
But he thought about playing
with Wally the next day.
And soon he was sound asleep.

Every day Big Bird and Wally
played together.
They played ball in the water.

They played follow the leader
on the beach.

They made sand forts
and tunnels.

And every day they shared
a cherry Popsicle.

Finally it was Big Bird's
last day at Granny's house.
It was a cold, rainy day.
Wally came to say good-bye.
Big Bird felt sad.
It felt almost like being homesick.

"I will write to you," Wally said.
"I will write to you, too,"
Big Bird said.
Then the rain stopped,
the sun came out, and...

a rainbow lit up the sky.
Wally and Big Bird ran out.
They played until Granny said,
"Time to go, Big Bird."

Then she said,

"Come back next summer."

Big Bird said, "You bet I will!"

3